S0-ABA-784

POLAR BEAR HORIZON

SMITHSONIAN OCEANIC COLLECTION

For Tom, with all my love — J.H.

For Cristina de Los Angeles . . . love of my life — A.C.

Book copyright © 2007 Trudy Corporation and the Smithsonian Institution, Washington DC 20560

All rights reserved. No part of this book may be reproduced or retransmitted in any form or by any means whatsoever without prior written permission of the publisher.

Series design: Shields & Partners, Westport, CT
Book layout: Konrad Krukowski
Editor: Ben Nussbaum

First Edition 2006
10 9 8 7 6 5 4 3 2
Printed in China

Acknowledgements:
   Our very special thanks to Dr. Don E. Wilson of the Department of Systematic Biology at the Smithsonian Institution's National Museum of Natural History for his curatorial review.
   Soundprints would also like to thank Ellen Nanney and Katie Mann at the Smithsonian Institution's Office of Product Development and Licensing for their help in the creation of this book.

POLAR BEAR HORIZON

by Janet Halfmann   Illustrated by Adrian Chesterman

Soundprints
Where Children Discover...

4

In a cozy den under a big snowbank on the north coast of Alaska, Polar Bear and her two cubs grow restless. The cubs were born in late December, during the long, dark Arctic winter when the sun doesn't shine.

Now it is late March. Spring is coming to this world of ice and snow near the North Pole. The den is getting too warm for Polar Bear in her heavy white coat.

On a sunny morning, she pokes a hole in her snowy den and sticks out her head. Her black nose checks the air for danger. All smells safe, and soon the furry white cubs peek out.

The cubs have much to see in this new world of white. A flock of white birds called ptarmigans eat willow buds nearby as snowy owls fly above.

Two days later, Polar Bear leads her cubs from the den into the snow. She is hungry and thin because she has not eaten for months. But she can't go to the sea to hunt just yet.

She must wait for her cubs to adjust to the cold and to grow strong and fast. They run, tumble, and chase. They slide down snow slopes on their bellies. *Whooosh!*

Then one morning, Polar Bear takes her cubs for a walk and keeps on going. The cubs put their paws in their mother's huge tracks as the family travels to the sea ice.

Above, noisy flocks of seabirds cry. They have returned from winter homes to build their nests along Alaska's coast.

At the seashore, Polar Bear walks slowly to let the cubs get used to the ice. Fur on the bottoms of their feet and bumpy pads on their toes help keep them from slipping.

As Polar Bear walks, she swings her head from side to side, sniffing the wind. She is smelling for seals. Before long, she smells the den of a baby ringed seal hidden under a snowdrift on the ice.

13

Huff-huff-huff-huff. Polar Bear grunts to her cubs, telling them to wait where they are and to be quiet. Then, slowly and softly, she pads toward the hidden den. Her cubs obey–for a while. Then the smallest cub scampers after her mother.

Polar Bear crashes through the snowy roof of the den. But the seals are gone. They heard the snow crunch under the cub's feet and have escaped into the water below the ice.

The cubs cry that they are tired. Polar Bear sits against a snowbank and nurses them with her rich milk. She bathes them with her tongue and holds them close while they nap.

17

When the cubs wake up, they begin to play. But play will have to wait for now. Polar Bear lumbers away through the snow and the cubs must follow. She needs to find food soon.

Polar Bear spots a big male bear in the distance. The male comes closer. Polar Bear growls and rushes at him. The big male turns and lumbers away.

On their way again, Polar Bear finds the breathing hole of a ringed seal in the ice. *Huff-huff-huff-huff,* she grunts to the cubs. This time, both cubs obey and wait quietly.

Polar Bear crouches above the hole. For a long time, she does not move. Suddenly, a seal pops up for air. Polar Bear springs and flips the seal onto the ice. Finally, she eats a good meal and the cubs taste the meat.

As spring melts into summer, the southern edge of the ice breaks up. The polar bear family moves north with the sea ice, leaping from one block of ice to another.

In an area of open water, Polar Bear teaches the cubs to swim.
To dry off, the bears shake themselves like dogs and roll in the snow.

Polar Bear shows the cubs how to creep up on a seal from underwater. She spots a bearded seal napping on the ice. Polar Bear swims under the ice and comes up right in the seal's breathing hole. *Surprise!*

25

Summer in the Arctic lasts only a few weeks. In August and September, the days grow shorter and colder.

One night, the cubs see something new. Beautiful northern lights glow in the dark sky.

In October, the first big blizzard of the winter hits. Polar Bear and her cubs curl up in a bed dug in a snowdrift. Blowing snow makes a warm blanket over them. In a few days, they are on their way again.

The cubs' first long, dark winter on the sea ice will not be easy. But they are ready. They now have a thick layer of fat to help keep them warm. And Polar Bear will keep their tummies full.

The cubs will stay with Polar Bear until they are two and a half years old. Come spring, they will try to catch seals themselves. Polar Bear will teach her cubs all they need to know to live on the sea ice at the top of the world.

31

About the Polar Bear

Polar bears live on the ice of the Arctic Ocean around the North Pole. The bears in this story belong to a group that lives on the Beaufort Sea, an area of the Arctic Ocean north of Alaska and Canada. There are more than 25,000 polar bears in the world.

Polar bears prefer to live near coastlines, where there are more open areas of water that attract seals. The bears use the ice as a platform to hunt ringed and bearded seals that swim in the water below. Bears find seals chiefly by smell, creeping up on them or waiting for them at breathing holes. In spring, polar bears hunt baby ringed seals in their birth dens.

Sometimes polar bears visit land. They may stay on land for months in areas where all of the ice melts in summer, such as in Canada's Hudson Bay.

Most females make their birth dens on land. They come ashore in fall and make dens in snowdrifts. The cubs, usually twins, are born in late December. They weigh only a pound and are blind and helpless. They grow fast, and by late March or April weigh about 25 pounds. Their mother then leads them from the den, and soon after to the sea ice. They stay with her for two and a half years, learning to be ice bears.

Polar bears are well suited for life on the ice. Their white coats help them hide in their white world. The hairs of their heavy fur are hollow to trap heat. In addition, a thick layer of fat keeps out the cold. This fat lets polar bears go without eating for long periods when food is scarce. Polar bears live 20 to 25 years.

Glossary

Arctic: Area around the North Pole, where it is very cold; winter days have 24 hours of darkness and summer days 24 hours of sunlight.

breathing hole: Hole cut in the ice by a seal so it can breathe air.

den: Warm, safe cave or other place where an animal can give birth or rest.

northern lights: Bands or rays of light sometimes seen in the northern sky at night.

North Pole: Point on the earth that is farthest north.

ptarmigans: Arctic birds that are white in winter and have feathers on their feet.

snowy owls: Arctic birds that hunt by day and nest on the ground; males are white and females are spotted or barred with dark brown.